A Cold
Goodbye

Ned Fain, Private Investigator
Book 1
A Hard-boiled Mystery

Sam Abbott

Sam Abbott

A Cold Goodbye: Ned Fain, Private Investigator, Book 1
Copyright © 2015 by Liz Dodwell
www.lizdodwell.com

Print ISBN-10: 1939860229
Print ISBN-13: 978-1-939860-22-4

Published by Mix Books, LLC

Table of Contents

One

I didn't plan on going to the zoo that day. It just sort of happened, but like my old mother used to say, there aren't any coincidences in life; you end up where God puts you, and then you decide for yourself what you're going to do about it.

I'd gone to a job interview at the parks office, hoping to get into something that paid better and wasn't as boring as house painting; but sometimes, you meet someone and just know right off the bat that he's a fake, that no matter what he says, he's gonna be lying. The guy doing the hiring, name of Stanley, was one of those. As soon as I shook his hand I could tell that there was something off about him, and within minutes I knew I was right. He got a phone call from one of his bosses who wanted something taken care of right away down in the camping area, and he told one of the workers hanging out there to go do it. About ten minutes later, while he was telling me what a great place it was to work, that guy called in to say that someone had busted a fence, and it was gonna take all day to fix.

Stanley called his boss back to deliver the bad news, and when the boss got ticked off, Ol' Stan threw his own guy under the bus, telling the boss that he figured his guy broke the fence and was just trying to blame it on the campers. Took me all of five seconds to realize I was at the wrong place, and I got up and walked out without saying a word.

Trouble was, the bus wouldn't be around for another forty five minutes, so I had to kill time. The zoo was right there next to the bus stop, so I wandered in for a few minutes. I always liked animals anyway, 'cause you can expect them to act like animals. People act like animals, too, but usually when you least expect it. I prefer to know who I'm dealing with, so animals get my vote for reliability.

I wandered around for a few minutes, and then saw a bunch of kids over by the polar bear habitat, oohing and aahing at the big white monsters as a zoo worker tossed fish over the fence to them. Kids are another bunch that tend to act real, so I stood a short distance away to watch with them.

The bears were doing their thing, going after the fish and even fighting a bit over some of the bigger ones, and the kids were getting a kick out of it. The big glass wall between us and them was crystal clear, so we could see everything, and the water line for the bears was about half way up the glass. The underwater part of the show was probably the best part, in my opinion, because those big, clumsy creatures were as graceful as birds, in the water.

I noticed the teachers there with the kids. One was a short, pretty little thing, the kind I always liked, and the other was an older lady, probably getting close to retirement age. The cute one whispered something to her buddy, and when the old gal nodded the cutie wandered off. I went back to watching the polar bears.

Ten minutes later the cutie hadn't come back. The kids were still engrossed in what the bears were doing and I was just about to go on my way, maybe go check out the elephants, when there was a big splash in the water behind the glass. I stared at what had caused it, trying to convince myself that I was seeing things, but I wasn't. It was a man, and he hit the water like a ton of bricks and just lay there, kind of half-floating.

I could tell from past experience that the guy was dead. No one alive would have just laid there in the water, not with four tons of meat eaters staring at him. And if he'd been unconscious, the shock of hitting that icy water would have been enough to at least make him stir, trying to wake up and figure out where he was.

Not this guy, though; he didn't even react when one of the bears chomped down on his arm and tore off a chunk. Dead, just like I'd said to myself.

The old teacher let out a scream, and turned away to bury her face in her hands. That left about forty little kids, maybe third graders, all staring at the glass while three polar bears ripped a man to shreds, and I knew that it would scar them for life if something didn't happen fast.

If I'd thought about it, I would have said it wasn't any of my business and left them to the zoo folks to deal with. Trouble with me is, I don't always think before I act, so I stepped up close and started herding them away from the glass.

"Okay, kids, let's go! Time to move on to see what the elephants are doing!"

A couple of the kids were screaming, and one of them looked at me. "But that guy, he fell in and the bears..."

"Calm down, that isn't real," I said loudly. "I work here, we're filming a scene for a movie, that's a dummy we made to look that way! They weren't supposed to toss it in 'til you guys were gone, but some idiot didn't wait for my signal! Come on, now, we gotta get you out of the camera shot! Let's go see the elephants. Hey, teacher, you gonna help me out here, or what? Let's get the kids away from the movie set, okay?"

The cute one came running up just then, and she took one look at the bloody mess in the water, then looked at me. In a split second, she took in my scarred face, my limp, and then turned to look at the water again. I could see the shock on her face, but she held it together, grabbed the other teacher and pushed her toward me and the kids, then started backing me up.

"Come on, kids, this man is right," she said. "It's all a stunt for a movie, and they started it before they were supposed to, so let's go on down the way and see the other animals, okay?"

It was working, the kids were calming down, and we started leading them out of the area while zoo employees and security guards came rushing in. One of the guards told me to stop and stay put.

"I'm getting these kids away from here, idiot," I hissed at him, "and then I'll come back. I saw it all, but unless you want these kids to have to go to ten years of therapy at zoo expense, let me get them off somewhere else, now!"

He looked at the kids, then nodded at me. "Okay, but I want you back here ASAP!"

The teachers and I herded the kids off to where I could hear elephants trumpeting, and then a zoo manager showed up to take charge of them. He told me and the teachers that we had to go back to the polar bear exhibit, to answer questions, and once the cutie knew the kids were covered, she agreed.

There was a plainclothes cop waiting when we got back, and a couple of uniforms standing around off to the side with zoo people. I wondered why the zoo could get a cop faster than your average citizen could, but that wasn't the time to ask questions like that. He took each of us aside, one at a time, to ask what we'd seen. I let the teachers go first.

"Your name, Ma'am?" the cop asked the older lady.

"I'm Lenore Mitchell," she said, and he asked her what she had seen when the body hit the water. "Well, I wasn't really watching the glass, I was keeping an eye on the kids, but when I heard that big splash, I looked up and saw a man had fell in, and then one of those creatures started tearing at him, and I just couldn't watch. I'm afraid I sort of panicked, and looked away, and then this man," she pointed at me, "he started telling the kids it was all part of a movie or something, and we started to move them away from it all. That's really all I know."

The cop nodded. "Did you see the man moving or anything, trying to get away?"

"I really didn't see much of anything, I'm afraid. It was such a shock, you know, I really just didn't know what I was seeing, and I should have been paying attention to the kids..."

The cop moved on to the cute teacher. "Name?"

"Jo—I mean, Josephine Rosier, officer."

"Miss Rosier, can you tell me what you saw?"

She shrugged. "Well, I had gone to the bathroom, and got back after it all happened. I mean, when I got back, I saw that Lenore was all upset, and this man was trying to get the kids to move away from the glass. Then I saw the blood and everything, and that's when I realized there was a man in the water. And of course, that's when I saw what the bears were doing to him. I saw this man," she also pointed at me, "and decided he was doing the right thing, so I started going along with him, getting the kids away from it."

The cop looked over at me. Like the lady, he let his eyes roam over the scars on my face, and I could tell he was making his own guesses how I got them, but I didn't care. "This man?" he asked, and she nodded.

"Yes, sir. He was like, taking charge, and seemed like he knew what he was doing, so I just went along with him. He's kind of a hero, I think. He acted like a... a policeman, or a soldier, just took charge and acted instantly! If it weren't for him..."

"Yes, Miss, thank you," the cop muttered, and then it was my turn.

"I'm Detective Carlson," he said. "Name?"

"Ned Fain. I was standing here watching the polar bears when the body fell into the water. I realized immediately that the man was dead, and I know enough about polar bears to know they're vicious and will eat just about anything, so I knew what was about to happen. Only thing to do was try to get those kids out of here, try to ease the shock for them the best I could."

"Wait a minute," he interrupted me. "You say you could tell the guy was already dead?"

I nodded. "Yep. No reaction to the cold water, no movements, not even involuntary ones, and while his eyes were open, he obviously wasn't seeing anything around him. I've seen dead men before. This guy was dead, but I think he'd only been that way for a few minutes, maybe even seconds."

The cop looked up through the glass. "You're thinking the fall killed him? From what I see, it's only about fifteen feet or so. Maybe the shock of the cold water?"

I shook my head. "No. He was brain dead before he hit the water. If there's enough left of him, I suspect you'll find he was either shot in the head with a small caliber bullet, or punched with an ice pick."

He looked me in the eye. "You seem to know a lot about this sort of thing. You a cop?"

"No," I said, shaking my head. "Ex-army, JAG. I had to prosecute a lot of murders, and was trained in forensic evidence. There are tell-tale signs that a living person, even one who was badly hurt and couldn't fight or try to escape, should have displayed, and he didn't show any of them."

The cop nodded again, and I got the feeling it was part of his "Colombo" act. Most cops try to affect some common mannerism that makes them seem less threatening to a suspect, and I always called it that. Guess I watched that show in reruns too much as a kid.

"Then you're thinking this is murder?"

"It is, unless the guy might have hit his head on something that could cause death instantaneously. That's a stretch, though, because he didn't seem to have any visible head trauma."

Another nod. "Well, the zoo crew is getting the polar bears out of the habitat, so we can get what's left of the guy out of there. Hopefully, we'll find a wallet or some way to identify him..."

I gave a tight-lipped smile. "Let me make your job easier," I said. "His name was Caleb Armstrong."

That got his attention. "You know him?"

"Knew him," I said, "since he's dead. But yeah. We were in the Army together, he got out about a year before I did. We worked in JAG together. He's in... was in private practice, now, but I don't think he worked much. He married money; Adalina Di Bari. Far as I know the only legal work he did the past couple years was handling her investment properties and such."

He looked at me for a second, and I was impressed that he managed not to nod again. "Any idea who might want him dead? Assuming you're right, that is, that it's murder."

"None. I hadn't seen him in about a year; we don't exactly move in the same social circles."

Once again, he looked at my scarred face. "Can you tell me how your face got damaged?"

Damaged. I shrugged. "It's on record. I was prosecuting some high-level Afghan officers for war crimes and got fragged. Someone tossed a grenade into the latrine with me, blew off part of my right foot, messed up my hearing and left me with these lovely beauty marks."

He glanced down at my feet, then back to my face. "Seems like you're doing okay. You're a lawyer, then?"

"Not anymore. Courtrooms bring back some bad memories. Lately, I'm painting houses with a buddy of mine, but I'm hoping for something better. That's why I was here, I had a job interview over at parks and rec this morning. Wandered in here while I waited for the bus, and just picked the wrong time to do it."

There it was, the nod. I knew he couldn't keep from it for long.

"Okay. Got a number where I can reach you, if I have any more questions?" I gave him my cell number, and he wandered off. A moment later, I saw him walk into the polar bear habitat, through a door that opened in the side wall.

I'd been half watching the ME's people as they fished out the body parts. Caleb had been wearing Dockers and a nice shirt, and one of them had found his wallet. I saw the cop look at his ID, and nod. Of course. I turned to go, and the cutie was standing there, looking at me.

"I just wanted to thank you," she said, and then held out a hand. "I'm Jo Rosier. I feel awful that I wasn't here for the kids, but I thank God you were."

I took her hand out of politeness; I don't like touching people or being touched most of the time, but like I'd said, she was cute. "Ned Fain," I said.

"Yes, I heard when you told the policeman. Anyway, I just wanted to say thanks." She held my hand for a moment, and I was just about to pull it back when she leaned forward and stood on tip toes to kiss my scarred cheek. "Thanks," she said again, and then let go of my hand and turned to walk away.

I watched. If they'd had teachers like her when I was in third grade, I would have deliberately flunked out.

Two

I went home - I lived in a flop hotel, one that let me pay rent by the week, which was easier when I made day wages - and just kicked back to relax. I had a painting job to get to the next day, so I turned on the tube to one of the movie channels and cracked a beer.

The bad thing about seeing someone die is that it won't leave your mind easily. While I watched Chevy Chase drive a modified Ford across the country, I kept seeing the whole thing over and over again in slow motion.

Caleb had fallen from somewhere well above the enclosure. He'd hit the water pretty hard, so I was guessing that he'd fallen more than the fifteen feet the cop had mentioned, probably more like thirty feet or better. I didn't know the zoo's layout all that well, but I seemed to recall that there were VIP areas up above everything else. Since he was married to more money than anyone else in the city, I'd guess Caleb would have access to one of those spaces.

I let my mind wander through the whole thing. I remembered coming into the area where the polar bears were kept, and seeing all the kids there with the two teachers. The younger one, the cutie, she had turned to the older one and whispered something; probably about going to the can, that's what she'd told the cop. I recalled her walking away (and how nicely she did it), and how the other lady seemed to be bored. She hadn't really been watching the kids at all, in my opinion, and when Caleb had come crashing into the water, she'd been ready to run and leave them behind. Not someone I'd want in charge of my kids, if I ever had any.

I remembered thinking that I had to do something about the kids, and that I'd concocted the lame excuse about a movie, but hey, I was acting under pressure. For a guy like me who had to deal with PTSD I think it was pretty good! Sure, the kids would all find out it wasn't true when the news hit TV, but I hoped that, by then, they'd be able to at least convince themselves they hadn't seen a guy get eaten by big white monsters. Might save some of them from a psychologist's couch, anyway.

The cute teacher, Jo, had come back then, and it struck me that she'd been gone an awful long time for a potty break. I guess she might have had the runs, or something, or maybe there was a long line at the ladies' room. She'd come back just in time to see the first bears chomp on Caleb, and I have to give her credit for keeping her head together. If she hadn't started working with me, the kids might have panicked completely. But she grabbed the old gal and started telling the kids to listen to me. Cute, and with a cool head, to boot. Wonder how she'd feel about a date with a scarecrow?

Remembering all this wasn't hard for me. One of the things I'd always prided myself on as a kid was my terrific memory, and later in life I'd gotten interested in how to improve it. I'd learned tricks for filing away everything I see and hear, almost like saving it to a computer, so that I could play it back later and find out more about it. It had been a great thing to have when I was JAG; made it easy for me to keep track of testimony and evidence. More than once it had made it possible for me to prove a client either guilty or innocent, just because I could fit all the pieces together like a big jigsaw puzzle.

This wasn't my puzzle, however, and I didn't need to be rehashing it. I shoved it all aside and tried to concentrate on ol' Chevy making a fool of himself over Christie Brinkley.

When the movie ended it was getting close to four, so I started switching channels looking for a news story about Caleb. I found it about ten minutes later, a head shot of some pretty female reporter in front of the polar bear enclosure.

"Local authorities are trying to determine how a thirty nine year old attorney fell into this polar bear habitat today. Caleb Armstrong, husband of socialite Adalina Di Bari, was apparently killed by the animals when they mistook him for an intruder."

"No, he wasn't," I muttered at the TV. The scene cut to a woman, and a subtitle said it was the zoo Director, Debra Pugh. The reporter's voice came from off camera.

"Ms. Pugh, do you have any idea how this might have happened?"

The woman frowned. "Not at this time. Our security department is cooperating with the police investigation, but all we can say now is that Mr. Armstrong and his wife are great supporters of the zoo and we believe that he may have been in the VIP lounge, above the habitat, before he fell."

"And was anyone else there? Anyone who might have seen what happened?"

"As far as we know right now, he seems to have been alone."

The scene switched again, and showed Caleb's widow, Adalina Di Bari. She was standing there looking completely composed, I thought, unfazed by the knowledge that her husband was dead, and the man standing protectively beside her looked like he was a lot closer than the "family friend" he was captioned as. The widow talked to the reporter for a moment, saying how awful it was that Caleb had died in such a tragic way, and then she was gone.

The camera cut back to the head shot, and the reporter said that there would be more information as it became available. I switched back to the movie channel and got another beer while I heated up a pizza for dinner.

The next day was back to normal, me hanging onto a scaffold for dear life as I slapped paint onto the gingerbread of an old Victorian house. My buddy Jim, who was also my boss, knew darn well I had a problem with heights, but he always stuck me on the top floor jobs anyway. Someday I'll find a way to get him back for that.

I painted all day and was pretty tired by the time five o'clock rolled around. Jim paid me my hundred and twenty bucks for the day, and I caught a bus back to the flop. Another night in paradise, I figured, as I cracked a beer and snooped in my mini-fridge for something to eat. I needed to go to the store, but didn't feel like it at that moment, so I settled for a cold ham sandwich and some nacho chips. Dinner now fixed, I plunked down on the bed to watch more TV.

The news was on, and the lead story was about Caleb. Seems I was right, and the ME had concluded that he was dead before the first bear bit into him, so the police were now officially calling it a murder investigation. I wasn't surprised, of course, but I was delighted they'd gotten it figured out so soon. Most of the time it seems to take the police weeks to get that far. I guess his widow's money had them hustling.

The evening went smoothly for me, the way a half dozen beers will make it go. By the time I fell asleep, the whole Caleb thing was just a dim memory.

I wasn't scheduled to work the next day, so I made it to the grocery store to stock up on pizza and chips and beer, the main staples of my diet the past year since I'd gotten my medical discharge. I toyed with the idea of buying some steaks, but I wasn't sure of more work anytime soon, so I held onto most of the money I had to be sure of paying the rent for the next week.

I'd gotten the grub stashed when my cell phone rang, and I looked to see who might be calling. I didn't know the number, so I let it go to voicemail, and then checked it when it dinged to say someone had left a message.

"Mr. Fain," said a voice I recognized as the cute little teacher, "this is Jo Rosier. We met the other day at the zoo, when that man fell into the polar bear den. I need to talk to you. Please give me a call back at this number, as soon as you can."

I listened to it twice, and wondered what on earth she might want from me. Yeah, she'd given me a little peck on my cheek, but that was for helping with the kids, and I didn't have any delusions that she could have been attracted to my ugly puss. Ask any guy with facial scars, he'll tell you he knows exactly what I'm saying. Girls don't get flashed for a guy who's been smashed!

Like I said, I don't always think before I act, so I hit the call back button. She answered on the first ring.

"Hello?" she said, sounding anxious.

"Ms. Rosier, it's Ned Fain."

"Oh, thank you for calling back so quickly, Mr. Fain. Listen, I really need to talk to you, but I don't want to do it over the phone. Could we meet somewhere, like right away?"

I took the phone away from my ear and looked at it as if it was a bug or something, then put it back. "What's this about, Ms. Rosier?"

"Please, call me Jo, and I'd really rather not go into it over the phone. Let's just say I think I might need your help. Please? I can meet you anywhere you want. And I can pay you, if you'll help me."

Now, the last thing I want to do is get involved in some woman's problems, and it didn't take a genius to figure out what this gal's troubles probably were. She'd been at the scene of a murder, and now she said she needed help; doesn't take a rocket scientist, know what I mean? I was dead sure it had something to do with Caleb's death, and my best guess was that she was a suspect in the murder. No, I didn't need problems like that, which is why I couldn't believe my own ears when I heard myself say, "Sally's Cafe on Fourth Avenue, twenty minutes."

She gushed her thanks and hung up, and I stared at my stupid phone again. How do I keep doing such stupid things, getting myself involved in things that are none of my business? I went to the dresser and dug out a clean shirt and jeans, then hopped into the shower. Five minutes later, I was walking out the door.

Sally's was only a block away, and I got there with five minutes to spare, so I grabbed a booth toward the back and watched the door. She came in right on time, and spotted me easily since it was nice and bright in there. She slid into the seat across from me and smiled nervously.

"Thanks for meeting me," she said. "I wasn't sure if you would, but you were the only person I could think of to call, after the way you handled things the other day."

I shrugged. "No big deal," I said. "So what's the problem, or could I guess?"

She looked at me kind of oddly, then, but a slow smile came over her face a second later. "Somehow, I bet you can. Want to try?"

I grinned. "Cops called you in for an interview about Caleb's death. No one can prove you went to the bathroom, or maybe someone is saying they saw you up by the VIP floor, but they're telling you that you might be a suspect. Am I close?"

The smile stayed, but faded just a bit. "On the money. There was no one else in the ladies' room or around it, and some guy who works as a janitor thinks he might have seen me going up by the VIP box over the polar bears. I didn't even know there was a VIP box, let alone where it might be."

I nodded, doing my impression of the cop from the zoo. "And I'm guessing that they have somehow tied you to Caleb; that you knew each other. Right?"

She let the smile slip and looked away. "Yes. We'd been having an affair, one that had gone on for almost three months, but when I found out who he was, and that he was married, I called it off."

"Then why was he at the zoo the same time as you?"

She looked down at the table, and just then the waitress finally came over. "Hi, guys, know what you want?"

I ordered coffee, and Jo did the same. She waited 'til the waitress had walked away, then said, "He called me that morning, and wanted to meet with me, said he'd decided that he loved me and was going to get a divorce from his wife." She raised her eyes to meet mine. "I know I should have told him to get lost, but he sounded so serious, and - well, to be perfectly honest, I really am - I was in love with him. If he'd really been John Bell, like he'd told me when we first met, I'd probably have married him within a week."

She swallowed hard, and then went on. "Anyway, he was supposed to meet me by the rest rooms, which is why I said that's where I was going. I'd told him my class was going to the zoo that day, and I thought it would be a nice, public place to meet. And with the kids along, it would provide sort of a cover, you know? Trouble is, he didn't show, and I figured he'd gotten tied up and couldn't make it, so I came back. I didn't know that was him in the bear house until I heard you say his name to the cops."

I sat there and weighed the odds that she wasn't involved in Caleb's death. I didn't like what I was coming up with.

"So what's any of this got to do with me?" I asked her.

It was her turn to shrug. "You said you were in the JAG office in the Army, so that means you're a lawyer. I think I need one, and while I might not know you, I know you're a good man, or you'd never have helped with the kids. I can go through the yellow pages, or I can ask the only lawyer I know who seems to be a decent guy. Tell me which one you'd do."

"Good point," I said, "but for one little detail: I'm not a lawyer anymore. I don't practice, and I was never a defense lawyer, in any case. I was a prosecutor."

"But - I checked the Bar Association, they said you're a member."

"I am. When I first got out, I started to go into practice doing corporate law, but - see my face? Last case I was involved in was prosecuting some Afghan officers for war crimes, and it got me blown up when I left the courtroom to hit the latrine. I lost part of my foot, about half of my hearing, and got all this beautiful cosmetic surgery out of the deal. When I go into a courtroom now, I get nervous, and it messes with my ability to think."

A light came on in her eyes. "PTSD. I understand."

"God, I hope you don't," I said. "Anyway, I'm not the guy you need, and before you ask, no, I can't recommend anyone. I'm out of the game, and I don't go around the field."

Her shoulders slumped. "Okay. I'll just try to find someone else I can trust then, I guess." Suddenly she looked up at me, and I saw a light go on again. "Wait a minute. If you can't help me as a lawyer, then how about another way?"

I narrowed my eyes, sure I wasn't going to like whatever came next. "Like how?"

The waitress brought our coffees and walked away, and Jo leaned forward to talk softly to me. "Look, I'm betting that Caleb was killed by his wife, someone she hired to do it. It was probably over his affair with me, and that would make sense why she'd want to do it when he was meeting with me. She must have known he was going there to see me, and sent someone to do it!"

I thought it over and agreed it could make some sense. "And? What can I do about it?"

"If you could find proof that would clear me, right? Look, if you were a prosecutor, then you must know how to investigate a crime. I've got money, my dad was pretty well off, and he left me a small fortune when he died last year. I could hire you to be my Private Eye and find a way to show that I didn't do it, and she did!"

I stared at her like she'd gone nuts, which she had. You don't hire a beer drunk to try to prove your innocence on a murder rap, and she was offering to do just that! Okay, yeah, she didn't know I drank a case of beer most days, but still, I wasn't a Private Investigator, and I couldn't take her money.

She wasn't done. "I can give you ten thousand right now, as a fee, and if it takes more than that, I can pay it as you need it. Please, Mr. Fain, I don't really know anyone here, I've only lived in the city about six months. I need help from someone I trust, and you're about it!"

I was already shaking my head as she spoke, ready to turn her down, but when I heard "ten thousand" my head moved in an odd circle for a second, and then I was nodding. Part of my brain began screaming at me to back up and say no, but my mouth opened up and this is what fell out of it:

"Call me Ned. Ten thousand is enough for a retainer, but it will probably go higher before we're done. I don't know what kind of experts I might need, and I probably will have to get some equipment..."

She broke into a smile. "Ned, I can't thank you enough, and you can call me Jo! I'm so scared about this.

You read all the time about innocent people getting railroaded for crimes they didn't commit, and without your help I could be one of them!" She took out a checkbook and began writing, and a moment later I was holding a check for ten grand, all made out to me.

I looked at it, then up at her face. "I'm gonna have to go to your bank and cash this. It's good, right?"

She laughed, and I could tell that her faith in me was taking a lot of the fear away. I hoped it wasn't misplaced. I promised to call her each day and left her with the tab for the coffee. Rotten thing to do to a girl I liked, maybe, but since I didn't think I really had a chance, it didn't matter that much.

On the other hand, if I was able to clear her, then maybe I could play on the whole "knight in shining armor" thing and get that date, after all.

Three

My first stop, as I told Jo, was at her bank. When I showed the teller the check and then presented my ID, she had to get a bank officer to okay the transaction because of the amount of the check, and I had to fill out a stupid form to say why I was getting the money in cash.

Sure enough, the check was good, and I left the bank with two fat pockets full of hundred dollar bills. I hailed a cab and had it take me to the local buy-here, pay-here car lot, where I dropped two grand on the down payment for a six year old Mustang. The car was in good shape, and someone had done some work to the motor, so it had plenty of power, and I just plain like Mustangs. After I got insurance and tags, I was free to drive around on my own, something I hadn't done since my discharge. To be honest, it took me a bit to get comfortable driving through the city, but I managed.

My next purchase was a smart phone. My old cell was an antique that I'd had for years, and I decided it was time to upgrade so I could make use of all the new technology. I had my number switched to the new one, and spent a half hour letting the sales girl teach me how to search the internet on it. That would come in handy now and then, I figured, especially when she showed me how to use the GPS to get instant directions to anywhere.

I went back to the car and headed for the zoo. I thought that would be a good place to start my investigation, get a look at the VIP area, see if I could find anything to tell me whether my client had been there. I parked in the admin building's lot and walked inside to where a security guard sat at the main info desk.

"Can I help you, sir?" he asked.

"Yeah," I said. "I'm Ned Fain, and I'm an attorney, working for Miss Jo Rosier. The police are calling her a potential suspect in the murder of Caleb Armstrong, and I'm interested in looking at the crime scene."

The man looked at me strangely for a moment, but then shrugged. "No problem, the cops are all done there. Let me get someone to escort you." He picked up a walkie-talkie and called another security guard to come and show me the way.

This one was a woman, and she wasn't bad to look at, but I wasn't interested in flirting. She led me around the back way to the stairs that went up to the top floor, slowing down for me as my bad foot made it hard to keep up. We walked about a quarter of a mile altogether, and I was hurting by the time we got there.

"The cops are saying someone killed him, and then opened that window to push him out." She pointed to a window at the front of the little room, and I walked over to look at it. It had a simple latch on it, like any window in a house, and I tried it. It opened easily, and the tall window that went almost from floor to ceiling slid aside like it was greased regularly, which it probably was.

"Do you know if they found any sign of a struggle? Anything out of place, or chairs overturned?" I indicated the several chairs that sat there.

"Huh-uh. Nothing was disturbed, and they said there wasn't any sign of blood or anything. They won't tell me why they think it's a murder, but to be honest, I think the guy just might have had a heart attack and fell, or something like that."

And that, ladies and gentlemen, is why security guards are not police officers. I studied the room without asking any more questions, and like the cops I found nothing. From that, I began to wonder if they had any evidence at all, but they must have found something to make them think Jo could have done it.

Motive? Yeah, if she was lying about having broken up with him, and he had called to tell her he was cutting her off instead, then she might have been angry enough to kill. Opportunity? If no one could corroborate her story about being in the can, then she might have had opportunity. The only thing left was means, and all I had on the murder weapon was my own guesses. Did she carry a small gun? Maybe a .25? Somehow I doubted she'd be packing an ice pick around with her. However, the fact that there was no obvious damage to his head or body before the bears got to him had me convinced it had to be something tiny, along those lines.

The guard's theory just didn't hold water, simply because a heart attack is almost never instantly fatal. No matter how bad it is, the victim is usually alive for at least a few minutes, even if the heart itself stops, because there is still oxygen in the brain. Until the brain is starved for oxygen it should continue to function, so hitting the water should have caused some sort of reaction, at least an involuntary contraction of muscles. Caleb hadn't moved at all; ergo, he was already dead, his brain non-functioning.

I thanked the guard and followed her back to the admin building, my foot screaming by the time we got there. The explosion that had done all the damage had completely removed the fourth and fifth metatarsals and their related phalanges (the two far right toe bones) from my right foot, and severed the tendon that connects to the heel, so all of my weight was concentrated on only about half of my foot. On top of that, I had to wear a brace to keep my foot perpendicular to the leg. Long walks made it hurt, and this one was pretty long.

When we got to the office building, the front desk guard called me over before I could walk out the door. "Ms. Pugh would like to speak with you, if you have a moment."

"Sure," I said, and he indicated a door to his left. I went to it and rapped on it softly and a woman's voice called, "Come in."

I stepped through and saw the zoo director. I remembered that her name was Debra Pugh, from the news story the night before, and introduced myself.

"Thank you for giving me a moment, Mr. Fain. I understand you're working for the woman the police think killed Mr. Armstrong?"

"Well, they haven't made an actual accusation, yet," I replied, "but she's been told that she is a suspect. She retained me today to look into the matter."

"I see. I really hope that she didn't do it. I knew Mr. Armstrong and his wife, of course, since they are generous contributors to the zoo's financial welfare."

I nodded, my new "Colombo" tactic. "Then I'm assuming he would have had access to the VIP area?"

"Oh, yes. Because of their support, they had their own key code for the door. The police asked me the same thing, of course, and wanted to know if that code had been used on the day of the incident. I checked for them and it had been, but there's no way to know whether it was used by one of them, or someone else they might have given it to. They were known to let friends use it from time to time."

That was interesting. "I'm curious, Ms. Pugh, why a zoo needs a VIP box. Surely the polar bears aren't so fascinating that people sit there for hours to watch them, like they do in a sporting event or a play."

She smiled at that. "The VIP lounge isn't actually for watching the animals, Mr. Fain, but it's provided to major contributors and visiting VIP's as a place of quiet and privacy. It's only coincidental that it ended up over the polar bear exhibit; I think it had to do with keeping construction costs down."

I filed that in my memory banks to think about later, but it immediately made me ask another question.

"Was Mr. Armstrong a regular visitor to the zoo? Did he use that quiet, private space often?"

Suddenly the woman's eyes were wary, and I wondered why. She looked at me as if she were wondering whether to answer, or how, then said, "Well, I wouldn't know that. As I said, we never knew who was using their key code."

I thanked her and promised to call if I had any more questions, and invited her to do the same. We stood and shook hands. I was silently thankful that I'd gotten to sit down for a few minutes, then walked across the parking lot to my car.

I couldn't really think of anything else to do, so I headed for home. As I parked the Mustang right in front of the building I wondered whether it would still be there in the morning.

That thought reminded me that I needed to call Jim and let him know I wasn't going to be available for a few days. I told him I hated to let him down, but something had come up that required my attention, and he accepted my excuse with only minor complaints. I told him I'd call when I was ready to paint again.

Hope he wasn't planning to hold his breath 'til then.

I went inside and looked into the fridge, then went back down to the car and drove to the Denny's out by the Interstate. I always liked Denny's, and I hadn't been to one since I'd gotten back so I decided to treat myself to a decent meal.

One of the best things about Denny's is that you can get breakfast all day and all night, so I had the Grand Slam with everything. I relished every bite of the eggs, sausage, bacon and pancakes, washing it all down with coffee, and suddenly realized that I'd broken a nearly year-long tradition; I hadn't cracked a beer as soon as I walked into my room. Maybe I would stop drinking; at least while I was working on this case. If I could, I'd probably start to think about trying to pull my life back together again.

All that could wait, though. For the moment, I was just enjoying the feel of a full stomach that didn't have a ton of triglycerides in it.

I hung around Denny's for a couple of hours, guzzling enough coffee to float a small boat, I'm sure, then went on back to the flop. While I'd been sitting at the restaurant, I'd thought of a way to protect the car. There was a big parking garage just a block away, one of the ones where you pay to park, and it seemed worth it to me to put the thing where there was security. I drove to it and got a ticket, then put it in the first spot I found on the lowest floor. The walk back to the flop only took about four or five minutes, and wouldn't have hurt if I hadn't already walked so far at the zoo. I got inside, opened the fridge out of habit and looked at the beer inside, then shut it and went to sit on the bed and watch reruns of Supernatural.

I dozed off after about the fourth episode and dreamed that Jo was a demon who was out to steal my soul. I was awakened from that nightmare by the sound of my phone ringing, and realized that it was already morning. I checked the phone and saw a number I didn't recognize, but answered it anyway.

A recorded voice told me that I was receiving a call from the county jail, and then paused to let the caller say a name. It was Jo, of course, and I accepted the call.

"Ned?" she said, frantic. "Ned, I've been arrested for murder! They came and got me early this morning, and say they've got evidence that I killed Caleb, that I stabbed him through the left ear with a knitting needle!"

A knitting needle hadn't occurred to me, but it would certainly fit, and going through the ear would make even less of a mess. "Calm down," I said to her. "Have they set a bail yet?"

"No, I'm supposed to be arraigned in about two hours. They just got me booked in, and this is the first chance I've had to call you. Oh, Ned, I'm so scared! I've never been arrested before, never been to jail! Is there anything you can do?"

"Not until they set bail, and then it will depend on how much it is, and whether you can afford it. What all are they telling you?"

"Just that I'm being charged with capital murder, and that I could get the death penalty! They say I went into the VIP place and killed Caleb, then pushed him out the window to try to cover it up by making it look like the polar bears killed him."

I nodded, then mentally slapped myself for it. "Okay, then just hang tight. I'm going to come and see you as soon as I can. Let them think I'm your lawyer, for right now. I'll see what's going on and fill you in when I get there."

I heard a sob through the phone. "Okay. Thank you, Ned. I don't know what I'd do if I didn't have you out there."

She hung up, and I got up and showered, then dressed in my one and only suit. A look in the mirror told me it was time to replace it, so I went and got the car and drove to the mall. It only took me about a half hour to buy a pretty decent one off the rack at a men's store, and I changed into it in their dressing room, stuffing my old one in the bag and then shoving bag and all into a trash can.

When I got to the PD I had to ask four times for whoever was in charge of the Caleb Armstrong case, and I wasn't too surprised when I was ushered in to see Carlson, the same plainclothes cop from the zoo. He looked up at me with some surprise, and then smiled as he remembered where he'd seen this mangled face before.

"Looks like house painting is paying pretty good these days, eh?" he said by way of greeting, and I shook the hand he offered.

"Not so much, no, but I got shanghaied into playing lawyer again for a while, so I thought I should try to look the part. I understand you arrested Josephine Rosier for Caleb's murder?"

He nodded. Of course. "Yep. We got her dead to rights. She killed him over an affair, stuck him with a knitting needle that we found in a trash can not too far from the scene."

I was taken aback at that. "Got her prints, or DNA on it?"

Carlson's eyes suddenly took on a guarded look, and I saw that he was looking off to his right as if searching for what to say. In law school, I'd learned that this is a pretty good indicator that someone is about to lie to you, so I just sat there in silence and let him hang himself.

"Yeah," he said. "We got prints, and when we searched her place this morning, we found a dozen more needles just like it."

I knew he was lying about the prints. Getting anything more than a partial from a knitting needle would be almost impossible, and I didn't see it as likely in this case. Whoever did the deed would have wiped it clean, I felt sure. They were basing their entire case on the fact that Jo had knitting needles of her own, and I'd bet they weren't even considering any other suspects at all.

"I'm gonna go out on a limb, here," I said, "and make a wild guess that the knitting needle you found is probably pink. Am I right?"

He looked to the right, but then looked me in the eye. "Yeah, it was. So what does that mean, that she's a feminine killer?" He laughed at his own wittiness, and I nearly spit in his face.

"No," I said. "It means the knitting needle you found is exactly like about a million others I could find in this city. So unless you really do have either prints or DNA evidence, which I know you don't, or got a confession out of my client, which I'm certain you didn't, I don't think I'm going to have too much trouble getting this case thrown out of court."

Carlson stopped laughing for a second, then guffawed again. "Boy, I'm glad you stopped by today! I haven't had a good laugh like that in years! There's no way it's gonna get thrown out, because she did it! So put that in your pipe and smoke it, Mr. Lawyer!"

I didn't rise to his bait. "Detective, with what you've got, I can not only get it thrown out, I can get you cited for dereliction of duty for making an arrest without sufficient evidence to back it up. Then I could file a lawsuit against you personally, and the police department, for wrongful incarceration and malicious prosecution, and my client would end up wealthier than Armstrong's widow. Care to make a bet with me on that? Now, I'd like to visit my client, if you don't mind."

Carlson's laugh had died out as I spoke, and the look he gave me made me think of the men who'd thrown the grenade into the latrine with me, but I didn't let it rattle me.

"She's at county," he said, and then turned back to his desk, dismissing me as if I didn't exist.

I got up and left, then drove out to the new Justice Center, which is what they call the county courthouse and jail complex now. I had never been there, and had to use the GPS on my phone to find it, but I got there only twenty minutes later. I went inside and told the jailer I was there to see Jo, and the woman told me that Jo had just come back from her arraignment. I got to wait for about a minute, then they told me to follow another jailer to the attorney visiting room.

I got there first, and had a seat on one of the two chairs in the room. Attorneys are allowed to meet with clients unsupervised, so when they led Jo in, the jailer unfastened her handcuffs and then closed the door behind her. She ran to me as I stood up, and threw her arms around my neck.

She said something I couldn't make out. I have hearing aids, but unless I can see a person's lips move, it's usually just noise to me, so I pushed her back and said, "What?"

She looked at me funny for a second, then relaxed. "Oh, your hearing," she said, and I nodded. "I said I can't believe you really came; right now it seems like I don't have a single friend in the whole world! I got the word a little bit before they took me to court that I've already been fired by the school board, even though I haven't been convicted of anything!"

"Yeah, that's just politics. Once we get this cleared up, they'll apologize and offer you a raise. How did it go in the arraignment?"

She sniffled, and I saw that she'd honestly been crying. "The judge set my bail at two million dollars," she said, and I sat down again. "They said since I'm not from around here that I'm a flight risk, but where could I go? I don't have any family living anywhere, and I know enough to know you can't hide from a murder charge, not for long, anyway."

"True," I said, "but that's not how the prosecution sees it. Did they say anything else, like about indictment?"

She nodded. "Yes, the prosecutor said it's going to the Grand Jury tomorrow, and he's confident I'll be indicted for Murder One. He already said he plans to go for execution, if I'm convicted. Oh, Ned, I just don't know what to think! Am I going to die?"

"Not likely," I said, "or at least not over this. This state hasn't had an execution for more than twenty years, and there have been a lot worse murders than this one. The right-to-lifers would get on this case and protest until the governor gave in and commuted you to life instead, but let's try to avoid having to count on them." I told her to sit down across the table from me, and began laying out what I'd learned at the PD.

"That clown Carlson has the case, and I've already got him shook up. They're saying you killed Caleb with a knitting needle, and that they found several like it at your place."

"Yeah, I knit, have since I was a kid. It's something my mom taught me before she died when I was ten. It relaxes me, and I usually do it after I'm done grading homework and tests. It's a stress reliever. Sheesh, I carry it around with me sometimes, like a security blanket."

"And did they tell you that they found a knitting needle just like yours at the scene?"

"Yeah, someone said that."

"Carlson tried to tell me they got your prints off that one, but I know he was lying. However, if it was yours, then DNA will say so, because when you touch something, you always leave traces of skin or body oils on it. And no, I'm not saying that means you did this. I'm saying that if you're right and the wife did it, then it's just possible she's gone to some lengths to frame you for the crime, and stealing a knitting needle from your place might not be that hard to do. Have you seen any sign of a break-in, lately?"

She thought hard. "I can't say I have, but then again, I come from a small town. A lot of times I come home after school and find that I walked out and left the door standing wide open, just forgot to close it or lock it. I guess it's possible someone could have taken one of my needles without me even realizing it. I hadn't thought of that, I just insisted it couldn't be mine."

I thought about it. It was possible that she was telling the truth, and it really was the wife who'd had Caleb killed. What I needed to do was establish whether she had motive, and that would take a visit to the widow to find out.

"Okay. I'm going to work on that angle, but it's time for you to get yourself a real defense lawyer. I can only do so much without going into court, and that just isn't something I'm prepared to do. Did you look any up?"

"No, but a couple of them gave me their cards at the arraignment. I guess I can call one of them." She looked glum, and I found myself wishing I could help her more, but going into court just wasn't in my cards, at least not anytime soon. Just thinking about it too hard gave me the shakes.

"Do that, then, and let me know who you get. I'll work with them to get this cleared up as soon as we can. And try not to worry too much. I think you're gonna be okay."

She got up and walked around the table as I rose, and put her arms around me, leaning into my chest. I was glad I was wearing a shirt, because the scars I had there were even worse than the ones on my face, and she probably would have pulled back in disgust.

"Thank you, Ned," she whispered, and then she tilted her head back and looked up at me. "If I'd met you six months ago, maybe I wouldn't be in this mess at all." She closed her eyes and pushed her lips up toward mine, and even though I was determined not to do it, I kissed her.

Scarred men should never fall in love. Something always goes wrong, and I was suddenly terrified that this was going to be one of those times.

Four

I left the jail and used my smartphone to find out where Caleb's widow lived. I'd seen her on the TV, and recalled thinking that she didn't seem too upset about his death; maybe the reason was because she'd arranged it. I couldn't wait to go and ask her, so I started up the Mustang and listened to my phone as it gave me turn by turn directions.

The house was in a very ritzy neighborhood, and I knew which one it was instantly, just by the ostentatiousness of the place. It had gates that were painted gold, for crying out loud, and the fancy lettering at the top said, "Di Bari Estate." I stopped at the gate and pushed the button on the intercom.

"Can I help you?" came a male voice.

"My name is Ned Fain. I'm investigating the murder of Caleb Armstrong, and I'd like to speak to Ms. Di Bari for a few moments."

"I'm afraid you'll need to call for an appointment," he said, but then a female voice cut him off. "Oh, let him in, for pity's sake, or he'll just start calling all hours!" A moment later, the gates began to swing open, and I drove on up to the enormous house at the end of the long driveway.

A man came out to look me over, and I recognized the family friend. He was of European descent, I could tell, probably Italian or Spanish, and built like a bull. I hoped I wouldn't have to prove I could kick his rear end, because I wasn't all that sure I could. He stared at me for a moment and I stared him right back, which must have been the right move. He grunted, and motioned for me to follow him into the house.

The place was as gaudy on the inside as it was on the outside. I tried not to show my distaste, but trust me, if I'm ever rich, like I win the Power Ball or something, I won't ever want marble statues of naked men and women in my front foyer. Gaudy!

I followed the bozo into another room, where the lady herself sat on a sofa waiting for me. She looked about like she had on the TV; aloof, unfeeling and like she'd just had botox injections in her entire face. There wasn't even the hint of any emotion in her expression, so I didn't know if she was happy, angry or just didn't give a rat's patootie that I was there.

"Mr. Fain," she said, still without moving any muscle except a couple around her mouth. I was going to have trouble reading her lips, I could tell, so I moved closer to try to hear as much as I could. "How can I help you?"

I took a seat without being invited to, in the chair nearest to her. I smiled and said, "I'm working for Josephine Rosier, the woman who's been arrested for your husband's murder. I wanted to ask you a few questions, and I appreciate you taking the time to see me like this."

She didn't say anything for a moment, just sat there staring at me. "You knew Caleb, didn't you? Didn't we meet you somewhere once?"

I nodded (Colombo style). "Yes, Caleb and I served together in the Army's JAG offices a few years. We got together after I came back to the city once last year, at Hanrahan's."

"Yes, I remember now. You were the one who got blown up. I guess that explains the scars."

Why is it that wealthy people think they don't need tact? I ignored the slur, if it was one, and kept smiling.

"Ms. Di Bari, can you tell me why anyone might want your husband dead?"

I got an expression then, because her eyebrows moved up the tiniest fraction of an inch. Even botox can't stop genuine surprise, I guess. "Why, I'm sure it had to do with that little whore of his wanting more of him than he would give her," she said. "Isn't that often the motive for a murder like this?"

I nodded again, thinking that I was going to strangle Carlson for giving me his stupid, subconscious habit. "It is, yes, but why would she kill him when he had told her he was going to get a divorce to be with her?"

The bozo was standing off to one side, and I caught his broad smile out of the corner of my eye, while the widow burst out laughing. "Divorce me?" she cackled. "Oh, my dear sir, if that's what she told you, then she is a very poor liar, indeed! Caleb wouldn't divorce me; he signed a pre-nup that guaranteed that he would get nothing if he ever did!"

"And you don't think it's possible that he actually loved Miss Rosier, wanted to be with her enough to give up all that your money could do for him? It's not that hard to believe; after all, Kings have been known to abdicate thrones for love. Why couldn't he have just wanted a simpler life with the woman he loved?"

"Obviously, Mr. Fain, you didn't know Caleb as well as you thought you did. He was not a man to whom the word 'love' meant anything but to be used as a ruse to get a woman into bed. If you doubt that, I suggest you ask any of the others he toyed with."

I thought about that for a moment. "You're saying that he had other affairs, besides Miss Rosier?" That might explain Debra Pugh's sudden insistence that she could never know if Caleb had been at the zoo.

"Oh, good heavens, yes! Dozens, possibly even hundreds! I didn't care, as long as he didn't let it become a scandal, and he knew it. He usually had several on the string at once, and he'd tell me which one he was going to see on any given night. Unless there was a pressing engagement that required his presence, we kept up the pretense that he was working on something and would simply be out late while doing so."

"And you didn't mind his infidelities?"

She looked over at the bozo. "Why would I? Rico was always here to keep me company. No, I'm afraid that Caleb was merely a convenient camouflage. He'd done some legal work for me when he'd first come home from the Army, and made a pass at me. Since I knew he could keep his mouth shut about certain things he handled for me, and since my family was so unforgiving of anything they consider 'unseemly,' like my relationship with a man of dubious ancestry, I married him with the understanding that we would be a couple in the public eye, but Rico would share my bed. He was free to spend my money, within some reason, and could use it to maintain himself in women of his taste. It was business, pure and simple."

"Then why the pre-nuptial agreement? What did it matter to you if he ran off with someone else?"

"Why, image, good sir! When you are wealthy, everything is about image! How would it look if my husband were to leave me? I made sure that doing so would cost him his slut-laden lifestyle, and he was quite happy with the whole arrangement."

About image... I thought. Yeah, more like about trying to outshine everyone else! "And if a scandal had occurred? If someone found out about his affairs and made them public?"

Her face clouded for a moment, but then she smiled again. "Then, depending on the circumstances, I might have divorced him. However, though we did face a couple of near misses, it never happened, so it wasn't an issue."

I caught that. "Near misses?"

She sighed. "There were a couple of women who thought they could blackmail him into leaving me. They threatened to send me photos if he didn't, and when he refused, the photos did arrive in my mail. A quick settlement, arranged by Rico, solved the problem on both occasions."

I looked at Rico, and he smiled. It was like looking at a happy shark who'd just invited you to dinner, and I could easily imagine him "persuading" a woman to give up and take the cash.

"So, just for kicks, what would have happened if one of those ladies had gone public, sent the pics to a newspaper or TV station, instead of to you? Would you have been the forgiving wife?"

She gave what sounded like a snort. "Hardly. Our agreement was simple; if he brought shame to the relationship, I could divorce him with only a minor settlement for his comfort."

"How minor? Are we talking a few hundred bucks, or a few hundred thousand?"

She hesitated, and I knew I was onto something she didn't want to admit to, but she knew I could get a court order to open that pre-nup, under these circumstances, so she might as well be straight with me.

"If I filed for divorce, the agreement was that he would get two million dollars, paid out over a five year period. It's a common clause for someone of my stature when entering into a marriage of convenience."

I let that digest for a minute. Somehow, I couldn't see this woman parting with two mil, not when she could just let things go on as they were. Would she divorce him for falling in love? Nah, she'd just tell him to keep it all under wraps and have fun!

That being the case, what motive could she have to kill her husband, or have him killed? I thought back through the conversation, and came up with the answer:

Image!

I decided to go for broke, and hoped it would not be me that got broken. "Okay, now that I understand this situation better, here's what I'm thinking. I think Caleb really did care for Miss Rosier, and really did tell her he would leave you, but that would ruin the 'image' and make your life hell. So I think you had Rico, here, follow them around a while. He figured out that the girl was a knitter, slipped into her house while she was at work one day and stole a knitting needle. Guy like Rico, he'd know that a slim weapon like that would be effective, and so when he followed them to their next meeting place - the zoo - he saw an opportunity to kill two birds with one stone, if you'll pardon the expression. A knitting needle into Caleb's ear and a toss to the polar bears, and then leave the needle where it can be found, complete with my client's DNA all over it. Sound good?"

Di Bari had sat there stone faced the entire time I'd been talking, while Rico just stood in the same spot and smiled at me. When I finished, they looked at each other, and then back at me.

"Mr. Fain, you have quite an imagination, but I'm afraid you're completely wrong. Rico was right here with me the day Caleb died. We never left the house."

"Can anyone else verify that?"

"Of course. Speak to my maids, or the chef. We were here the whole day, until the police called to tell me what had happened."

I nodded, taking it in. I was pretty sure her staff would know that keeping their jobs (and probably their health) would mean saying whatever the lady wanted them to say, so that wasn't going to be much help. I thanked her for her time and rose to leave, then turned back at the last moment before walking out of the room.

"One last thing, Ms. Di Bari. Do you knit?"

That frozen face took on an expression that made it look even more like ice. "Mr. Fain," she said in a hoarse whisper full of insult, "do I look like a woman who would need to make her own clothing? Good day, sir."

Rico walked me out. As we got close to my car, I looked over at him. "So, you ever do any leg breaking for the lady? Or maybe something more permanent?"

He stared at me with that same shark-tooth smile for a long second, then said, "Not yet." He watched me get in and drive away before turning back to the house.

I thought about my next move as I drove back into town, and decided I needed to know more about the case against Jo. I decided to go to the DA's office and find out what I could. I knew where it was, right there at the Justice

Center I'd left an hour before, so I headed back the same way I'd come.

The prosecutor on Jo's case turned out to be an old schoolmate of mine, Igon Ybarra. While I'd gone to Harvard Law, Igon had attended the State University and gotten his law degree there. We hadn't been buddies in school, and in fact, he'd been one of the bullies that picked on all the weaker kids.

He'd never picked on me, but I suspected he was about to start. When I was ushered into his office, he looked up and visibly recoiled from my appearance.

"Igon, how ya been?" I asked as an opener. "Ned Fain, in case the beauty treatment throws you off."

He looked at me for a moment as if trying to remember, then smiled a fake smile. "Ned Fain! I remember you! I heard about what happened to you, man, really sorry about that. Happened in Iran, right?"

"Afghanistan," I replied. "But that's nothing. I'm here about a client, Josephine Rosier. You've got her on Murder One for Caleb Armstrong."

His face went back to showing distaste. "Yeah, the knitting needle killer! I'm going to fry that girl. She's about as cold-blooded as they come, managed to sit and cry like she didn't know anything all through the interview!"

"Well, I'm not so sure about that, Igon. Seems to me that your evidence is pretty circumstantial, and I think we can show that a frame-up would have been easy. I've got other suspects with both motive and likely opportunity, and they're slick enough to put the blame on the girlfriend. So unless you've got something I'm not aware of yet, I think this case is not gonna be the one to make your career."

Igon did a fair impression of Rico's shark smile. "Well, then maybe that bomb did more damage than just messing up your face. See, I've got a lot more than that. Your little client was seen going up to the private box that morning. I've got a witness who puts her there about five minutes before splashdown! Now, how does that sit with you?"

I shook my head. "Igon, if you'd keep up with current studies in evidenciary science, you'd know that eyewitness testimony is about the most unreliable evidence you can present to a jury. Out of all the cases where someone is sentenced to death or life in prison for murder that have been overturned by DNA evidence, over seventy percent of the convictions were obtained based solely on eyewitness testimony that proved to be wrong. If that's your strong point, our legal team is going to rip it to shreds."

He was about to protest that I was crazy, I'm sure, when my phone rang. It was Jo, and I accepted the call from the jail.

"Ned," she said, "I got a lawyer. Her name is Katherine Miller, and I told her about you, so she wants to talk to you as soon as you can."

"Okay, I'll give her a call as soon as I get done where I'm at now. How you holding up?"

She sighed into the phone. "It's not as bad as I feared," she said. "They put me in with a girl who's about to go to prison for dealing cocaine, and she's actually pretty nice, so that helps. I just hope I'm not here for too long, and can get back to my life."

"That's what I'm working on, kid. I think we're looking good."

Jo started to say something I didn't catch, and then changed it. "Ned - when this is all over, do you think you might want to get to know each other better? I mean, don't get me wrong, I just - I've never known a man like you, who will do so much to help someone like you're doing. I think I'd like to see if maybe..."

I caught myself nodding, and stopped. "I'd like that," I said, and then we hung up. I looked back at Igon.

He was all puffed up by then, like a bantam rooster in a barnyard full of hens. "I'm confident of my witness, and by tomorrow I'll have DNA from the knitting needle that will put it in your client's hand. Add in the fact that she was having an affair with one of the most well-known Don Juans in the city, and we've got a pretty solid case."

I shook my head at him. "Let me give you another scenario. Caleb's widow, Adalina Di Bari, is a cold fish. She's got a boyfriend who probably has a rap sheet as long as your ego, and if she divorced Caleb she'd have to pay him off to the tune of two million bucks. I'm thinking she had the boyfriend, Rico Potenza, follow Caleb and my client, steal one of her knitting needles, then wait for the next time he caught them together. A quick jab with the needle, a toss out the window to the polar bears, leave the needle where it's sure to be found, and you've got a perfect crime."

I struck pay dirt, and I knew it. Igon was looking off to the right, desperately trying to find something to say that would shut me down, but it wasn't there. My scenario was good enough to cast reasonable doubt in the minds of any jurors, and he knew it, so all he could manage to do was get mad and tell me to get out of his office.

I left, and called the new lawyer from the hallway outside his office. She told me that she'd just gotten off the phone with Igon's clerks, and was expecting a copy of the prosecution's file any minute, so why didn't I come on over? I got the address and said I'd be there as soon as I could.

Thank goodness for GPS! Her office was downtown, and I got there in about thirty minutes, mostly because traffic was backed up behind a wreck on Main Street.

Katherine Miller was a nice looking lady, and she greeted me warmly. I think Jo must have warned her about my face, because she only glanced at my scars for a second before offering me a seat across her desk. I thanked her and sat.

"So," she began, "I just got the file, and frankly, it doesn't look to me like they have much of a case. The eyewitness is a janitor at the zoo, and from his picture he looks like a tweaker."

A tweaker is a meth-head, someone who's addicted to methamphetamine. The drug is one of the most devastating in the world and does strange things to the minds of its users. They tend to be paranoid and extremely delusional, and it's very easy to manipulate them into doing or thinking what you want them to, as long as you're careful not to anger them. It wouldn't be hard to get such a person to insist and even believe that they'd seen what you want them to have seen, even if they weren't really in the vicinity at the time.

"That's good for us," I said. "What about forensics, anything there?"

She shook her head. "Not much, I'm glad to say. They sent the needle off for DNA analysis, but I'm inclined to think that they'll find hers on it. She told me your theory about someone stealing a needle from her to use in a frame job, and it makes sense to me."

"Yeah, well, I got even more than that, now." I told her about my visit to the grieving widow, and how my theory was taking on solidity, and added in my entire conversation with Igon. She nodded thoughtfully.

"I know him, he's probably the weakest prosecutor in the whole office. I can't imagine how he's kept his job there for the past five years, because he hasn't ever won a conviction on a major case. To be honest, I'm surprised his boss let him have this one; it's got potential for political oomph, if they can convict her, just because of who the widow is."

"True. So what else they got?"

She shrugged and passed me the file. It wasn't very thick, and I read through it in about ten minutes. The more

I read, the more sure I was that Jo had been set up, and that Adalina and Rico had done it. The last item in the file was the transcript of Igon's interrogation of Jo right after her arrest that morning, and I read through it slowly, looking for anything that might hurt our case.

And I found it.

Five

I left Katherine's office and went straight back to the jail to see Jo. When I got there, they took me to the same visiting room that I'd been in with her before, and then brought her in a few moments later.

She smiled as wide as you can imagine when she saw me, and as soon as they took off her cuffs, she rushed over to throw both arms around my neck. Her lips met mine instantly, and it was a kiss like I hadn't known in years. I let her go with it for a moment and just enjoyed it.

Jo was the kind of woman I dreamed about when I let myself imagine a life with someone to love. She was sweet, smart and lovely, and a part of me wanted to know if she really would give me a chance, if there might be romance in my future with her.

The problem with that was that I am, down under everything else, utterly honest with myself. That's something I learned from my old mother, too, that a man must be honest with himself at all costs, or he can never trust himself to be honest with anyone else.

That honesty forced me to accept the probability that Jo was making such offers only to keep me on her side, keep me working hard to get her freed from this dangerous predicament she was in. She didn't need to trick me; I had accepted her money, and my sense of self honesty made it imperative that I do my best to get to the truth.

Sometimes that came back to bite me, though.

Jo let go of me and sat down when I motioned for her to, still smiling at me like I was her long lost love. It hurt me to see that smile, knowing that it would probably be the last time I ever saw it. She must have seen the pain in my face, because her smile began to fade a bit.

"Ned," she said, "what's wrong? What's the matter?"

I looked at her for a long moment, and I recalled how I'd had a premonition that something would go wrong if I let myself care for her. That premonition was coming true, and as much as I hoped that there was a way out, I knew better.

"Jo," I said, and then had to regroup my thoughts. "Jo, when you called me this morning to tell me you'd been arrested, you said that the cops told you that they had evidence you'd killed Caleb by stabbing him through the left ear with a knitting needle. Remember that?"

She looked confused for a moment, then nodded. "Yes, that's what they said. Why?"

I felt my heart breaking, but I didn't let it show. This was going to be hard enough for me to do without letting myself feel it at the same time.

"Jo, I went and met with your new attorney this afternoon. She's smart, and she's good. She managed to get the prosecutor's preliminary file within an hour, and that isn't easy to do." I cleared my throat. "So, anyway, I went and talked with her and we agreed that you were probably framed. Then she showed me the whole file, and I got to read through it."

She looked interested, but a little wary. "Okay. And?"

"The only witness they've got is a known drug user, so discrediting him would be easy. And as for the knitting needle, I gave your lawyer enough info to make it a no-brainer to get a jury to believe you were set up. She agrees that there's little chance that you could ever be convicted on what they've got, so without something else, like a confession, you're pretty much home free."

Her face lit up like a thousand candles. "Ned, that's wonderful! Oh, my God, how can I ever thank you? Ned, I just..."

I held up a hand to stop her before she went any further. "There's just one thing that's bothering me, Jo. Like I said, I read through the entire file, and one of the things in it was the transcript of the recording from your interrogation this morning. Remember when Mr. Ybarra came in and started yelling at you, trying to make you confess to the crime?"

She nodded, but didn't say anything. I think she was trying to figure out where I was going.

"Well, I read through it pretty thoroughly. In the beginning, Ybarra asked you your name, address, all that, and then he asked you if anyone had already talked to you about Caleb's murder. Do you remember what you said?"

She nodded. "I said that some cops had asked me where I was when it happened, and that they asked me a few other questions."

It was my turn to nod, but it wasn't a Colombo thing, this time. "Yeah. And then he started asking you about the murder itself. He told you that he was charging you with First Degree Murder, and he read you your rights. You waived them, and said you didn't have anything to hide, remember?"

She nodded again.

"He told you that Caleb had been killed by a knitting needle, and asked you if you were a knitter. You said you were, and he held out a knitting needle they'd taken from your house during the search, while you were being arrested, right? He told you that they'd found a knitting needle just like it in one of the trash cans near the entrance to the polar bear enclosure, and asked you point blank if you stabbed Caleb in the ear with a knitting needle. You said no, you hadn't, remember that?"

"Yes."

"At that point, Ybarra said that he was going to see about your arraignment in order to get bail set, and then he walked out of the room. The recording ended then, and the clerk took it to type it all up. Now, all of that is fine, that doesn't hurt your case a bit."

She was watching me cautiously. "Then what's the problem, Ned? It's all going to be okay, right?"

"Unless they get something a lot more solid, yes. You're going to walk. But, you see, Jo, the problem is that I know you did it."

Her eyes went instantly wide, just as I'd expected them to do. She stared at me for a moment, then said,

"What? Ned, come on, you can't be serious! I told you, I'm innocent! Ned, I want to get this over with so we can try to make a life together, don't you want that?"

I nodded. "I would love it, Jo. The trouble is... the trouble is that I could never get the fact that you murdered a man out of my mind, so there's really no hope of that ever happening, now is there? Let me tell you what I know, okay? Here's how I see it."

I looked her in the eye and ticked off points on my fingers as I described them.

"First, you lied to me when you said you had broken off the affair weeks ago. It was still going on, and the zoo was where you often met, because the private VIP box was a safe place for some afternoon fun.

"Second, you were telling the truth when you said Caleb called and asked to meet you there that day. What you lied about was what he wanted to say; it wasn't about divorcing his wife, it was about cutting off the affair with you.

"Third, you slipped away from the other teacher and the kids to go meet him in the box, but when you heard what he said, you lost it. You were in love, and he was breaking your heart and destroying the fantasy of life with him that you had built up over the past few months.

"Fourth, you reacted without thinking. You instinctively reached for the one thing that you always turned to when you were stressed out, your knitting. But when you saw the knitting needle in your hand, you didn't want to create something with it, you suddenly wanted to

61

destroy. You didn't even think about what you were doing, you just reached out and stabbed at Caleb, and the needle pierced his ear easily.

"Fifth, when he fell and you realized what you'd done, you panicked. You knew no one would believe you that it wasn't intentional, so you thought about how to cover it up, how to distance yourself from it. You looked out and saw the polar bears down there, feeding on the fish that were being thrown to them. You thought that if Caleb were to fall in there, he'd be attacked and eaten, and there wouldn't be any evidence that he was killed in the box at all. That would get you out of the line of fire.

"Sixth, you opened the window carefully and saw that no one could actually see up to where you were. It took all your strength, I'm sure, but you got Caleb back into something like an upright position, and just let him tumble forward. He fell right through the open window, and you shut it instantly, then hurried down the stairs and back to the kids.

"The one thing you didn't count on was me. Because of my experience as a JAG Officer, the cop took me seriously when I said Caleb was dead before he hit the water, and that's why they looked closer at what had, at first, seemed to be only a tragic accident. They found the needle and thought it was odd. Then the autopsy found that his ear and brain had been pierced by something just that size, and two plus two always makes four. They looked deeply enough to connect you to Caleb, and the rest is history.

"That's how I see it. Want to tell me if I got any of it wrong?"

The woman across the table from me was suddenly different from the one who'd come in. I couldn't put a finger on it, but her entire demeanor had changed, and it was like I was looking at an entirely different person, suddenly.

"Are you wearing a wire?" she asked me.

"Nope. This is between you and me, Babe."

She smiled again, but it was a different kind of smile than I'd ever seen on her face before.

"How did you figure it out? I thought I had everything covered, and you were so good at coming up with theories that worked."

"When I read the transcript, nowhere in the interrogation or questioning did anyone tell you that Caleb had been stabbed in the *left* ear, but you'd known it when you called me this morning. The only way you could is if you were there when it happened, and only Caleb and his killer could have been there."

She chewed on her lip for a second. "You missed a couple of things," she said. "Most of it went like you said, but then when I heard you talking to the cops, I knew I was in trouble. That's why I called you and begged for your help. I needed to make you believe I was innocent, but I also needed to make it impossible for you to ever testify against me. You're a lawyer, so I had to hire you. Attorney-client privilege, remember? Once you took my money, even if you figured it out, you couldn't reveal it to anyone. I'm not stupid, Ned, and maybe even a little smarter than I look. It worked; I got you hooked and paid you, so there's no way you can tell anyone what you know."

I nodded. "True. If you had hired me as your attorney. Trouble is, you didn't. You hired me as a private investigator, something an attorney can do but which is not covered under privilege. There's nothing to prevent me telling anyone that you just confessed to murder."

The smile vanished. "No, you're a lawyer! I can complain about you misconstruing the facts about how I hired you, and anything you say will be thrown out!"

I shook my head. "Sorry, Jo, but even your own attorney knows you hired me as an investigator. That's what you told her, and if she's asked, she'll have no choice but to confirm it, since your call to her from the jail would have been recorded. The prosecutor could easily get a copy of it."

She stared at me for a moment and began to cry. "Ned, come on; yeah, okay, I did it, but it wasn't deliberate, I didn't mean to! But what about us? I wasn't lying about that, I really do feel some connection between us, don't you? Don't you want to give us a try? A chance?"

"Jo, I'd love to, but like I said, I'd always remember that you killed a man. I can't live with that. I'm sorry."

She looked down at the table. "Well," she said, "what are you going to do now?"

I looked at her, and truly wished things could have been different. I reached into my shirt pocket and pulled out the digital recorder I'd gotten from Ybarra moments before coming in to see her.

"I'm going to turn this over to the prosecutor, Jo, and then I'm going to go home and try with all I've got in me to forget about you."

She stared at the recorder. "But you... I asked if you were wired and you said you weren't! I'd never have said anything if I'd known..."

I shook my head. "Jo, Jo," I said, "did you really think you were the only one in this room who could lie with a straight face?"

I walked out and let the jailers in to take her back to her cell. I could hear the names she was calling me all the way back to Ybarra's office, and I can't say they didn't hurt, but I wouldn't let them stop me from doing what I knew was right.

Besides, I should thank Jo. She dragged me out of the pit I'd been in, and showed me how to maybe come back to life.

Being a PI would beat house painting, any day.

The end

If you enjoyed this story, please leave a review. Your words really mean a lot.

Get a FREE *unpublished* Ned Fain story and be among the first to hear about Sam's new book releases and special deals when you join his email list here:

http://www.mix-booksonline.com/sam-abbott-insiders

More adventures with tough, sometimes cynical private eye, Ned Fain:

The Electric Axeman
Ned Fain, Private Investigator, Book 2

Of Two Minds
Ned Fain, Private Investigator, Book 3

The Texas Hold'em Deaths
Ned Fain, Private Investigator, Book 4

A Poisonous Mind
Ned Fain, Private Investigator, Book 5

Beyond Betrayed
Ned Fain, Private Investigator, Book 6

Get books 1-6 in a set for just $2.99:
Ned Fain, Private Investigator Books 1-6:
A Cold Goodbye and Other Stories

Sam Abbott

…is a pseudonym for a popular author of adventure and cozy mystery. Who is that, you ask? Well, that's another mystery.

Join Sam on his facebook page:
https://www.facebook.com/SamAbbottAuthor

If you enjoyed this book, you might also like these:

- Adventure/Mystery – **The Captain Finn Treasure Mysteries:**
  - The Mystery of the One-Armed Man
  - Black Bart is Dead
  - The Gold Doubloon Mystery
  - The Game's a Foot
- Adventure/Mystery – **The Agency Confidential series:**
  - Deceit
  - Cheat

www.ingramcontent.com/pod-product-compliance
Lightning Source LLC
Chambersburg PA
CBHW071207130626
46555CB00004B/1608